God Talks to Me

Blessings,

[signature]

A Collection Of Poetry "If a Soul could Sing"

God Talks to Me

...to encourage the weak,
to strengthen the grieving,
and to give your heart 'Wings'!

DIANE RANKER RIESEN

TATE PUBLISHING
AND ENTERPRISES, LLC

Published by Tate Publishing & Enterprises, LLC
127 E. Trade Center Terrace | Mustang, Oklahoma 73064 USA
1.888.361.9473 | www.tatepublishing.com

Tate Publishing is committed to excellence in the publishing industry. The company reflects the philosophy established by the founders, based on Psalm 68:11,

"The Lord gave the word and great was the company of those who published it."

Book design copyright © 2015 by Tate Publishing, LLC. All rights reserved.
Cover design by Eileen Cueno
Interior design by Manolito Bastasa
Photograph of the tree courtesy of Maria Wahl Photography

Published in the United States of America

ISBN: 978-1-63449-764-0
Poetry / Subjects & Themes / Inspirational & Religious
15.02.19

There are so many family and friends that deserve a sincere 'thank you'. This collection of poetry came from the many experiences in life that I've had with all of them. We are all in this world together and go through so many of the same feelings. We have moments of great happiness, and also times of deep sorrow. I pray that somewhere in these pages of poetry, each of you will feel God talking to YOU, too!

With Love,
Diane Ranker Riesen

Contents

Preface

I never really intended on putting my poetry into a book. I've always written them to help myself or someone I love whenever any of us were going through a hard time. Many of my friends and family persuaded me to get a lot of them together and publish them. I hope they can help you also.

Many of them are 'praise' and happy poems because I know that God is the 'main' reason I've been able to handle the sorrows that we all go through in life. He has lifted me through all of them. I still have so many questions; but, I know that I will understand some day.

You will find poems that seem to call out for help. I understand how hard it is to stay positive even when you have a strong "Faith." I lost both of my parents young, my sister young, three babies; and the list continues. I truly know how so many of you are feeling when you are so discouraged and sad. It helps to know that you are not alone; and I think you will be able to feel that in a lot of my poetry.

I want to thank so many of my family and friends for all of their help and love throughout my entire life. None of us can handle everything alone. We need the prayers and care from others. My faith has been mentored and strengthened by so many of you. Two incredible mentors to me are Senior Minister Paul Barnes and his wife, Diane Barnes of Madison Christian Church in Groveport, Ohio and originally at Christ's Church in Tiffin, Ohio. No words can convey to any of you what your inspirations have meant to me.

I pray that this collection will bless you. I'm just like everyone else. God has helped me by giving me these words.

We all have a journey through life that will test us in many ways. I wish you all great peace.

Diane

A Meeting

If God showed at my doorstep.. and asked to come on in ~
If He would answer questions... where would I begin?
I guess, at first, I'd sit and stare... and question if it's real;
and then I'd try to talk to Him and tell Him how I feel.

I'd thank Him first for loving me, and giving me my soul ~
I'd run to Him and hug Him ~ I'd need for Him to know...
that everything I have and love is all because He's "King";
and that I'll try to honor Him... I owe him 'everything'.

And, then, I'd ask Him to sit down ~ and help me understand..
why there is so much pain around and never seems to end.
I think He'd gently hold my hand and lean in close to me ~
I think when I gazed in His eyes ~ such sorrow I would see.

I'd feel His heartbreak instantly; I'd sense His tender pain ~
Before a single word is said ~ I'd hug Him once again.
How could I really understand?... How could I really know?
I can't see things as God does ~ there's no way He could show.

A sense of calmness covered me ~ no questions even spoke;
His majesty secured me... and then my 'spirit' woke~
God's never wanted sorrow ~ He hates the tears we cry;
He promised us our freedom.. His compassion showed me
   "Why".

A perfect world is wonderful ~ but we would never learn;
Man's consequences follow us; and sorrow comes, in turn.
Although I'll always wonder…why pain and sufferings stay ~
I'm certain of God's perfect plan; I'll trust Him through
   each day.

                              Diane Ranker Riesen

A New Day

Photographer: Brenda Windau Pisani

A New Day

Although your walk seemed very long- with sorrow on
the way;
there'll come a time when light slips through.. you'll reach
a brighter day.
Sometimes those sad times through the dark, will never
seem to end......
But, just when you are giving up---- there's 'hope' around
the bend!

We're never guaranteed a life that's free from trials and pain-
Some days won't be so sunny … you'll have many filled with
rain.
Those rainy days are when we need…. to reach deep in
our soul;
And hold on to the truth that God will fill that empty hole.

When walking through the valley, when feeling lost and
torn….
Remember there will be a time you won't seem tired and
worn.
Our tunnel has an ending…. there's a time you will not
mourn ---
keep walking through, keep firmly strong… a 'new' day will
be born!

Diane Ranker Riesen

A Simple Tree

Photographer: Nadine Felton

A Simple Tree

(The Easter tree)

I started out a simple tree ~ with shallow roots to grow -
I thought my purpose 'simple'.. how little did I know.
The future held a plan for one such tiny piece of wood;
I hardly knew the task ahead; or even…if I 'could'?

One early morning, just past dawn…
some men came to my 'spot',
They started 'sawing' on me with the
tools that they had brought ~
and as my bark was cut away~ and
while my branches fell….
I wondered what they needed-- was
my wood, to burn, or sell?

The soldiers gathered up their work
and took me to a place….
where I was carved, cut, and prepared…
for Human's 'great disgrace'.
They laid my finished product ~ at the base of Calvary…..
I heard the people shouting that a man would die on me!

This man was forced to carry me along a path of pain ~
They nailed Him to my broken wood~ as I lay lost in vain.
They made Him suffer 'far too long',
I couldn't bear to see….
this humble man, so torn with blood…
was dying "there" on me.

If I could only soothe Him….. if only I could touch;
I'd wrap my arms around Him, for
He'd suffered long enough.
And while He shed His blood on
me ~ He shed it, too, for You~
He took your pain and sacrifice and did all He could do.

Then soon my shame was lifted..
as I saw His perfect plan…
He used me in a simple way~ to save the fate of man.
Great honor filled my broken wood….as I began to see…
I held the "King of Kings", just me ~~~~ an ordinary tree!

Diane Ranker Riesen

DIANE RANKER RIESEN

A Smile

There is nothing seen so brightly;
Nor a feeling quite so sweet—-
As the smiles that reach your vision
...from the people that you meet.

Diane Ranker Riesen

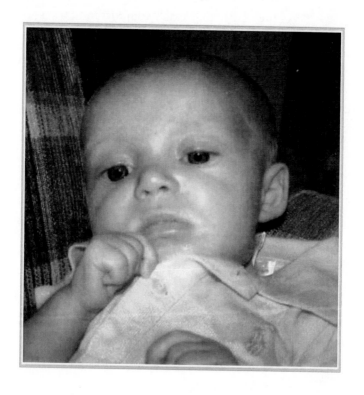

Angel Ava

Photographer: Nathan Nitecki

Angel Ava

Have you ever met a special soul…
whose heart was very rare ~
You knew that you were being
'blessed' - just by being there?
Your soul was touched far greater~ than
you ever thought it could….
You knew you loved her instantly,
and that you always would.

For those of us who knew her ~ Ava
was that 'special soul' ~
she changed our lives forever… in ways she'll never know.
And though her life was short in days,
you knew right from her birth;
that time can never steal away .. the
blessings she was worth.

God's trials can make us wonder, and
we'll never understand ~
But, Ava served her purpose; with each
moment that 'He' planned.
In God's own time we'll know the truth ~
and 'why' He took her home.
Her memories will comfort us ~ when we feel 'most' alone.

I dreamed the "Heavens" opened up ~
and heard the Angels sing ~
I saw the 'Joy' in Ava's face……. and saw her tiny 'wings'.
When I awoke, I sensed her near; and
knew that dream was real.
Life never ends ~ love never dies….
it lives in what we feel.

Diane Ranker Riesen

Angel Mine

Photographer: Lori Kobelt "The Icing"

Angel Mine

Where did thirty years go?
How could time move on?
Even though it's been so long….
I can't believe you're gone.

There are so many struggles;
and pains we all go through ~
But, nothing can compare…
to the truth of 'losing' you.

Most days seem fairly normal…
I've learned to hide so much ~
But never doubt, my soul still waits..
for the moment we can touch.

Broken dreams still haunt me.
Lost memories still hurt strong….
But it will all be worth it ~
When you're back where you belong.

I believe God's plan is perfect;
I know His love is true.
You were such a perfect angel…
I think Heaven needed you.

Some days I ache to see you….
And other days…pass by.
Some days I seem just fine ~
while other days, I cry.

But, in the end… I'll be with you ~
And, oh… what peace and joy….
When I can finally hold you,
and kiss my baby boy.

Diane Ranker Riesen

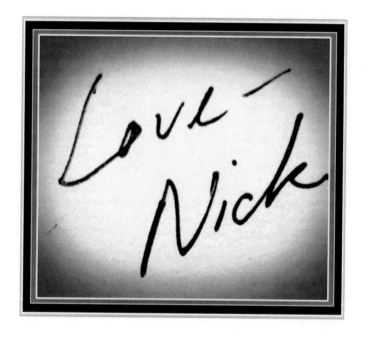

Another Chance

Photographer: Sarah Woodruff

Another Chance

(Nick's heart transplant)

God gave us each a life to live ~ His
plan was yet unknown,
We each had dreams of happiness
when we were fully grown.
Our lives were different and unique
as we lived out each day,
Who knew what turns our paths would
take, the struggles on the way?

I don't know how our future's formed
or how each life is planned~
why sorrows strike, and pain grabs
hold … I try to understand.
But I am no one special, just the same as all on earth;
I haven't earned a miracle, my life's of common worth.

And then there's 'you'; another soul,
a body blessed with health~
Your family's love and friendships filled
your life with countless wealth;
And then, as if the darkness fell, your
time on earth would end,
And still, before you left us, you became my 'Angel', friend.

Your heart beats now… inside of me; your legacy lives on ~
And I will try to honor you until my time is gone.
I can't explain your journey, or see God's perfect view.....
Perhaps you'd done His Will on earth,
and Heaven wanted you.

I won't forget your gift to me, I feel it beat within..
Before I fall to sleep at night, my prayers will each begin ..
That God surrounds your family with
a comfort none can see,
Your final earthly gift so pure.. You gave my life to me!

Diane Ranker Riesen

Answered Prayer

Artist: Jeff Seitz

Answered Prayer

When someone's time on earth is through;
and the moment's chance has past....
It's not the large and special times,
But,the small ones that will last.

We each have precious times to share;
and all the countless days...
But, in the end, the simple unknown moments -
light our way.

My heart still aches for those I've lost;
my dreams still strive to see -
But all the simple memories ~ ~
those times have lifted me.

Sometimes I wish I'd done much more ~
sometimes I want 'one' hour.....
To hug again, to kiss once more;
to send a simple flower.

But in those times, my loved one speaks
inside my lonely soul.....
And whispers words that heal my heart;
a gift so beautiful.

"Don't think of me with any pain;
don't carry one regret...
You loved me as I dreamed you would ~
A 'gift' I won't forget."

One night I prayed and asked my God,
"What does my loved one see?..
Can loved ones still surround my life? ~
Can they still nurture me?"

God's answer calmed my worried thoughts ~
He could not bless me more;
He told me they are near me....
and much closer than before!

Diane Ranker Riesen

Assurance

Artist: Christine Vera Mundschau

Assurance

Within the meadow filled with green ~
I rest upon your earth…
I take some time to clear my head; and
find the moment's 'worth'.
In those reflective minutes..as I gaze upon the ground ~
I look for God's great beauty ~ and find it all around.

The splendor of each wild flower comes bursting into view;
with rainbows full of color; and sweet
smells through and through.
They all reach up to touch the sun ~ and
spread such glorious leaves ~
and in these precious moments.. I'm assured why I believe.

Who else can make a flower? Who else can make it grow?
With all our human knowledge…. there's
so much that we don't know.
And as I see a butterfly glide softly through the air ~
I know that I am not alone~ and someone else is there.

He is the one who shines the stars;
and gives each life it's air~
He is the one who guides the night
and lingers everywhere.
I look up to the Heaven's with an awe I rarely feel……
and once again, I know for sure ~ that God is really real.

Diane Ranker Riesen

Autumn Rainbows

Photographer: Cindy Shuff Peacock

Autumn Rainbows

In yearly wonder, I gaze among the trees ~
The ever-changing rainbows… that live within
their leaves.
And God's great power comes to mind,
Amid the beauty ….. that I find.
How great the magic ~ in His hands;
To meet the needs each day demands.
How perfect can our Master be….
Who knew the way to make a 'tree'?
The change will mark a Summer's end;
As leaves fall softly to the ground…….
Soak in the glory Autumn brings,
And see God's glory all around.

Diane Ranker Riesen

Believe

If you believe that God is real, and you believe He's true ~
then that belief must stay alive each
time you're struggling through.
There are no guarantees that life will always go your way ~
but, holding strongly to your Faith…
will ease you through the day.

It's easy to be faithful when your trials are far and few…
But, oh, so hard to carry on when sorrow's chasing you.
God understands when you have doubt,
He knows the 'hurt' you feel;
His Son went through such countless
pain; He knows 'Your' pain is real.

Just hold on to God's promises ~ even when you're mad….
God gave us hearts to crumble; and feelings to feel sad.
But, in the end, when all is through ~
and all our lives are done;
We'll realize eternity, and the 'joy' that we have won.

Diane Ranker Riesen

Broken Dream

There are such times that stop our hearts;
and cause our breath to slow.....
Those moments so unbearable;
our fragile minds can't know.
In those deep, endless days of dark,
attempts to help will fail----
No earthly love can ease the pain; no comfort can prevail.

What can we do to carry on? What answer can there be?
There seems to be no solace; and no way to set us free.
A numbness creeps into our souls...
no distant signs of hope;
We pray God understands us;
and the way we need to cope.

For no more shall a single tear stream
down our swollen cheeks-
We shall stand firm and let no pain
of sadness make us weak!
No tortured anguish, tear filled eyes,...
we shall not show our grief;
For nothing can sustain us or give us some relief.

And then we pause and close our eyes,
and KNOW our loss is real...
Would it be better if we closed our hearts, and didn't feel?
God knows the truth is in between...
the numbness and the screams;
We can't ignore the loss we feel ~
from all our broken dreams.

We must take time for sorrow; we must take time to feel.
For we've lost a precious miracle-
only time can help us heal.
The greater that our love was; the worse our loss will be-
Our God lost His child also; and His love will set us free.

Diane Ranker Riesen

Can You Imagine

Photographer: Diane Ranker Riesen

Can You Imagine?

What happens when a loved ones dies ~
where does their spirit go?
I think that it would help me... if I could sense and know.
It takes such strength to keep your Faith
when so much is unknown ~
But, God must have a reason why
our answers are not shown.

Perhaps it's just too beautiful... too much for us to feel ~
Our joy in life is fleeting; but, in Heaven, it stays 'real'.
I can't imagine all the love ~ that perfect, sacred peace...
our souls renewed in glory... with joys that never cease.

I think God's plan is perfect ~ and
He knows we cannot know;
for if we truly knew the end.... we'd surely want to go!
God let's us feel a taste of what Eternity will be ~~~~
and then when "He" is ready... My God will come for me.

Diane Ranker Riesen

Choice

Tonight, as I lay down to sleep...
I have a choice that I can make ~
Should I be grateful for today ~
and keep the joy when I awake?
We all have different plans go wrong;
and other dreams that seem so far...
But the way we 'feel' will mold our day...
our "attitude" is who we are.

Sometimes it's just so hard to see...
why struggles crowd my day ~
But, if I keep on trying ~ somehow I find a way.
It's easy to be peaceful; when everything seems right...
but much harder to feel happiness..
when trials make you fight.

Yes, we will all have hardship;
and some days that make us cry ~
but then, there will be other days that show us why we try!
I'm going to say my prayers to God;
and then lay down my head....
determined not to fear my days...
but, love each one, instead.

Diane Ranker Riesen

Cleansing

Photographer: Debra Hoffman Gardner

Cleansing

A wearied soul upon the shore,
With empty hope of joy no more ~
Shall find a refuge in the sun
And bathe in Glory from the 'One'.

For dare we not to test His plan,
Or end before our time is reached –
The highs and lows of life shall come,
Just as the oceans' tides become.

Yet, lay in peace upon the sand,
Just close your eyes and take His hand.
His peace shall cleanse you, calm your fear ~
As waters wash your worries clear.

Diane Ranker Riesen

Cloud Joy

Photographer: Gloria Frankenfeld Stacy

Cloud Joy

On one, long, lazy afternoon ~ I went out to the yard;
I looked for something beautiful…. it wasn't very hard.
The grass was soft beneath me, and the
sky was filled with clouds ~
they seemed to look like people
speaking to me right out loud!

I thought I saw my grandma.. just sitting in a chair ~
the more I looked, the more it seemed…
like she was really there!
This cloud brought back my memories ~
of when she was alive;
and as the cloud seemed to disperse…..
another one arrived.

This cloud looked like an angel - and I soon began to cry;
I wished that I could reach above…. if I could only fly!
The angels wings were open wide ~ as if to wave 'hello',
and suddenly I felt content.. they saw me here 'below'.

Sometimes I think God uses things ~
to let us know "He's" there;
and on that day my soul was sure that He was everywhere!
I can't wait for another simple… quiet afternoon~
I may just spend some time tonight…
looking at the moon!

Diane Ranker Riesen

Dark Strength

Something's always missing now,
when I awake from sleep…
I used to be excited…but something's wrong down deep.
My heart has lost it's rhythm…. My soul has lost it's hope;
Where once my day was filled with dreams……
I search for ways to cope.

There's got to be an end to this ~
each day's unending pain;
Although the sun is shining bright…… all I feel is rain.
Does someone have an answer? ~
Will someone make it right?
I feel so weak and weary.. and I'm tired of the fight.

"My child, please hear me clearly…
and listen to my voice…..
I, too, have days when I can find NO reason to rejoice ~
But, I know something no one knows,
I know your lifetime's end;
And, though you feel it's hopeless….
I know it's NOT, my friend."

"I've loved you long before you lived ~
I know the strength you own;
Even at your darkest hours… please
know ~ you're not ALONE.
I am the one who made you; I know
that you are strong……..
Keep Faith while you are struggling…
I'm with you all along."

Diane Ranker Riesen

Deep Roots

Photographer: Pamela Riesen Stevenson

Deep Roots

I took a stroll inside a woods… and gazed upon the trees;
the air was crisp and cooler,
there were rainbows in the leaves.
I stood in awe and watched them ~
as they swayed within the air;
and felt a sense of joyous calm…as I was standing there.

Who knows what dreams were made
here… the wishes that were thought;
Who knows how many perfect pictures
all the leaves had caught.
The bark on every tree there ~
seemed so content and strong ~
It seemed they were placed perfectly;
and everyone belonged.

I tried to just imagine all the history that had past ~
If only there had been a way ~
I would have stayed and asked.
And then I felt a strength within each
mighty tree that stood…
All that nature brought them ~
and the rains that soaked that wood.

How mighty and majestic these trees revealed to me ~
Nothing stopped their growing... how
strong they seemed to be.
I felt God's power surging through
the branches of those trees -
I prayed their roots would always strive ~
and they would always "be"!

Diane Ranker Riesen

Did You Know?

Sometimes I sit and wonder ~
when I stop and think of you...
if you understood the love I felt;
and if you really knew.

They say that 'real' love needs no words ~
and hearts just 'feel' what's true;
But, still I wish I'd told you more....
the LOVE I had for you.

Did you really know just how I felt?
Were you certain how I cared?
Did you know how proud I was of you?
..... those special years we shared.

As I sat and wondered softly....
In the stillness of the night ~
I slowly drifted off to sleep,
and a sweet dream came to sight.

You stood there in such shining 'joy',
and quietly, I heard.....

"You showed me every minute, without a single word.....
I know how much you loved me,
...and know I loved you, too.
You gave my life it's 'purpose'...
I'll be waiting here..for you."

Diane Ranker Riesen

Emptiness

Photographer: Jeanne Ardner

Emptiness

Dear Lord, I need to feel You; my soul has disappeared…
I want to feel some comfort ~ I need something to hear.
I never dreamed there'd be a night..
when all my 'faith' seems gone….
I always seemed to sense you…. but,
tonight ~ there's something wrong.

I feel so broke and weary ~ and I'm trying hard to pray;
My mind is tossed with endless thoughts…
there's something in the way.
Oh Lord, I truly feel ashamed ~ I always felt You 'near'…..
But, in my broken sorrow… there's
no sense that You are here.

Just then, when I felt hopeless; and
I closed my eyes to sleep ~
I felt a stirring in my soul, a warmness soft and deep.
And then, as if by magic ~ I heard a voice inside;
His perfect words brought comfort
and my heart began to cry.

"My Child, I'm right here with you ~
and I know your pain is deep;
I don't want you to feel alone… I'll stay here as you sleep ~
Sometimes the pain is just so strong…
the hurt will block your soul…
you don't need to feel so bad ~ "that" pain, I've also known.

I had a time of doubt myself; and
called out for some peace ~
I felt so lost and weary… and the torment wouldn't cease.
Just close your eyes, My dear one….
I'll help you to get through…..
My promise is unending ~~~~ I'll 'always' be with you."

Just then I felt surrender ~ and I gave my pain in prayer;
I never was abandoned…. My Lord was always there.
I knew that I could fall asleep; as
God proved He was 'true' ~
God answered when I needed Him ~
and I would make it through.

Diane Ranker Riesen

Enough Love

Photographer: Sara Burgderfer Riesen

Enough Love

A mother often wonders, as her heart begins to search…
if she'll ever love another child ~ the way she did the first.
But, all those silent worries that stir quietly and wild…
are quickly proven useless ~ when
her eyes behold the child.

A mother's love is endless, no beginning and no end ~
there's enough to love whatever
blessings God decides to send.
And when I held you in my arms ~ this miracle so new…
I felt my heart melt slowly; as I fell in love with you.

A quiet boy by nature, ever thoughtful… so aware ~
endless feelings, deep and quiet… not
afraid to show you cared.
Your thoughts were seeking endlessly
for what is right and wrong.
It's 'minds' like yours who really care ~
that's where those thoughts belong.

You were always strong and able ~
always anxious to achieve;
in times of disappointment… you
would be the last to leave.
You stood your ground, and carried
on ~ no matter what the cost;
I knew you won each victory… when
others thought you lost.

I've watched you grow from boy to
man ~ so able now to start…
a new life's journey on your own…forever in my heart.
You'll make a difference with each day ~
your kindness will shine through.
Remember with each passing hour ~
my 'love' will stay with you.

Diane Ranker Riesen

Everywhere

When someone's time on earth is through;
and the moment's chance has past…
It's not the large and special times,
But,the small ones that will last.

We each have precious times to share;
and all the countless days…
But, in the end, the simple unknown moments -
light our way.

My heart still aches for those I've lost;
my dreams still strive to see -
But all the simple memories ~ ~
those times have lifted me.

Sometimes I wish I'd done much more ~
sometimes I want 'one' hour…
To hug again, to kiss once more;
to send a simple flower.

But in those times, my loved one speaks
inside my lonely soul…
And whispers words that heal my heart;
a gift so beautiful.

"Don't think of me with any pain;
don't carry one regret…
You loved me as I dreamed you would ~
A 'gift' I won't forget."

One night I prayed and asked my God,
"What does my loved one see?...
Can loved ones still surround my life? ~
Can they still nurture me?"

God's answer calmed my worried thoughts ~
He could not bless me more;
He told me they are near me...
and much closer than before!

Diane Ranker Riesen

Flying Angels

(Tribute to the Angels of Sandy Hook Elementary)

Fly high little angels ~ do not cry;
for none of your souls shall ever die –
No "evil" can steal our memories~
nor force us to ever say good bye.
Your imprints in life will never end;
as deeply our pain will slowly mend~
With each passing day ~ you'll touch our hearts..
For death cannot keep our souls apart.

We'll hear your sweet whispers in the wind,
As softly the breeze flows through our hair ~
So gently your laughter will be heard-
We'll witness your presence... everywhere.

Each Spring as the blossoms slowly bloom,
and carpets of green shall hug our lands ~
Your beauty will shine through nature's show,
amid the new scenes your life will stand.
We'll smell your sweet scent throughout the breeze,
As God sends the soft winds through the trees.

The warm sun of Summer sets you free~
Your innocent hugs will comfort me,
As always we'll feel your presence near~
And know that your life is always here.

Far out on the rolling waves we'll see.....
while standing upon our sandy shores,
Your faint, scattered wings dance lightly there;
to play in your freedom ever more.
The warm Summer rays of sunshine fall,
as soft billowed clouds enhance our view..
The glory of all your beauty seen ~~
each miracle shows a sign of 'you'.

The views of our changing Autumn days ~
display your sweet glory proudly seen,
With each changing color of the leaves,
as hues of the Fall replace the greens ~
Look closely at each moonlit night~
stare deeply at the darkened sky,
Amidst the stars our eyes shall view ~
the countless wings that fill our sight.

When gentle, sparkling snowflakes fall ~
to carpet lands with heaven's glow,
You'll dance upon each crystal star;
as Heaven's kisses drift below.
And they will add a wonder 'round ~
with sparkling dreams upon the ground.

Keep guard little angels... by our sides,
No evil can touch you ever more.....
Your shining innocence still abides ~
Until we meet at Heaven's door.

Diane Ranker Riesen

Forever Dream

Photographer: Linda Kraft Hoerig

Forever Dream

Can a dream come true.. if you dream real hard?
Can a wish that you want .. be real?
Are there songs in your heart ~ that can't be heard;
and joys that you may not feel?

Our lives are a magical, mystical ride ..
in a world filled with blessings untold;
There are millions of feelings just floating around ~
that are waiting for us to take hold.

Open your hearts to the beauty about..
Spread open your wings and fly.
Don't miss the sweet secrets that hide on your way ~
look closely as you walk by.

There's nothing so hard, that it can't come true....
There's no hopeless dreams in the night.
This world contains miracles in every day ~
Each struggle is worth every fight.

Don't give up your wishes, your hopes, or your dreams ~
Embrace every hour with a smile;
Despite any sorrows on dark, gloomy days ~
this beautiful world is worthwhile.

Diane Ranker Riesen

Forever Mine

Many years and thousands of days ~ as
many memories; in a million ways;
Just 'yesterday'… a wide-eyed boy …
to love, to hold, to just enjoy.
It seems these years have rushed right past ~
So quick… the days have moved so fast-

Yet, I remember every breath, each move
you made, and tear you cried ~
each ball you threw; those times you'd hide.
No power on earth can steal those times ~
each memory stays "forever mine".

From "boy" to "man"… transformed in view ~~
Then, before my eyes - a perfect "you".
I cherish every moment, and cling to every touch ~
and with each smile you gave me ~
New love grew, still…so much.

The years won't stop ~ although I've prayed ~
That every day would 'freeze' and stay;
I know your days will still go on ~~~
Then one day you'll be off and gone.

Enjoy your life and spread your wings ~
Grab all the joy that this world brings;
But, in some quiet moments 'stilled' ~
Keep strong your Faith … your spirit filled.

DIANE RANKER RIESEN

With every broken dream that's cast ~
And all the 'joys' that may not last....
When sunlight ends and the day is though;
Remember, I'll be here for you.

Diane Ranker Riesen

Forgiveness

I'm trying, Lord, please help me…
My heart feels so betrayed,
The anger that was spoken; and the accusations made~
"Forgiveness" is the hidden threat
that lurks within my soul;
I've tried to just ignore it ~ but, it swallows me up whole.

I want to be the kind of light that leads to rightful ways~~
And set God's good example by the way I live my days.
But, ~ 'forgiveness' stays elusive; and
will rarely show it's face..
I feel I've left my Savior down, I'm crippled in disgrace.

I need humbled by your words, Lord ….
please help destroy my pride ~
I need YOUR strength to do this;
I can't myself….. I've tried.

I'll close my eyes in reverence to the
One who holds my day;
In silence ~ listen closely….. to the words You have to say.
"My child, I gave MY son to you;
He came to show the way ~
Remember all the mocking; and
the unjust lies they'd say…

And yet, through all the pain he felt …
the torture on that tree;
He still forgave His killers;
so your souls could be set free."

I opened up my eyes then….. to a feeling of rebirth!
God had offered me 'forgiveness' ~
when I know I had no worth.
If the King of Kings could bow down
and forgive one such as me ~
How can I not repay Him by "forgiving" endlessly?

Diane Ranker Riesen

Freedom Flight

Photographer: Tom England

Freedom Flight

Fly upon my weathered wings …
up high where only nature sings ~
Where earthbound troubles fall away;
Where burdens never meet the day.

And stretch your soul into the light….
as we begin our "Freedom Flight".

A clarity of peace unknown…
is felt as nature's life is shown ~
Such simple joy… such quiet song;
Your spirit feels that it belongs.

You can feel the truths so near ~
the meaning of your life seems clear.
There are no magic dreams below….
to fill your heart and soothe your soul ~

Serenity is only found……
when no more earthly hopes are bound;
And YOU see life in 'perfect' light ~
take pause to find your 'Freedom Flight'.

Diane Ranker Riesen

From Heaven's Hand

Photographer: Toria Felton

From Heaven's Hand

Good morning, World! ~ another day
has sprung from Heaven's hand;
And, Oh, the joy of witnessing the beauty of this land.
Each space is such a miracle ~ a work of God's own art;
such awe and majesty displayed....
I'm lost at where to start.

A flower yawns good morning to the glory of the day,
and all of nature's wonders awake and start to play.
I step into the morning air ~ and
breathe the force of love...
I'm welcomed by the grass below; and by the sky above.

What countless blessings all around;
if I just take the time ~
to stop my thoughts and use my soul...
to hear all nature's rhyme.
For, nothing in the world compares.....
to what is given 'free'.
If we just pause with open eyes ~~~
and take the time to see!

Diane Ranker Riesen

God's Art

As deep as any ocean... too far to ever know ~
God's miracles are countless; His blessings overflow.
The sunlight bursts with happiness... the air feels fresh
   and clear;
and if we only take the time ~ we'll know that God is near.

The flowers bid a sweet hello... the birds fly gently by ~
I see God's beauty in a laugh; and see Him in a 'cry'.
His visions are around us ~ in everything we see....
God's work is in the meadows, in the waters, in the trees.

Just take a walk among his art; and breathe His mighty
   power ~
He smiles at us through every cloud... and loves us through
   each flower.
How beautiful our world beholds.... God's wondrous, perfect hand;
His artistry is breathless; and as countless as the sand.

I want to always take the time... to notice each design ~
and see how many miracles my daily walk can find.
The beauty that God brought us is like a quiet prayer.....
and if we look around ~ we'll see God's EVERYWHERE!

                                        Diane Ranker Riesen

God Still Makes Angels

Photographer: Annie Johnston
'mother of Charlie, Tommy, Grace & Haddie'

God Still Makes Angels

I used to think, when I was young…
that all the world was right~
there were no darkened moments,
each day was filled with light.
I believed that good was everywhere;
and saw the special things…
And often, when I looked around, I noticed 'angel wings'.

Some people say as we grow up, we lose the joy of youth~
the world takes hold as each year
grows; and we forget the truth.
I know when I was little, as I would gaze around….
at special little moments, there were 'angels' on the ground.

I used to mention what I saw… my
parents would just 'smile'.
They'd say I was a 'dreamer', and they'd humor me awhile.
Yet, no one can convince me… I know
those wings were real—
And as the world takes hold of you ~
such doubts will try to steal.

I still can see those angels… they
grow fainter with each year.
I hope I never get convinced … that they were never 'here'.
They say when you are younger; you
can see a clearer view…
That children see 'reality', and what is really true.

I miss those days of innocence, the
years have made them 'dim'~
when I could see God's miracles; I
miss that 'proof' of Him.
Then, just when I am troubled… and
I question what I knew….
I see another set of wings….. I saw them, there, on you!

Not everybody sees them, not everyone sees clear—
But, if you really look around, you'll see some angels here.
God still brings angels, now and
then… to live within our view;
I know I'm right, I saw your wings…
God sent us one through you.

Diane Ranker Riesen

God's Night

Who knew the power of His hand;
the mighty works that He had planned?
This world is filled with countless views ~
that show the miracles in YOU.

Each star is placed within the sky...
as golden beams of moonlight fly;
the night-sounds whisper all around ~
as countless sights of life abound.

The night air wraps my heart, and soon...
a brilliant light comes from the moon;
and I am awed by all God's power ~
His magic in the evening hour.

I stay and gaze upon the show ~
the beauty dwelling 'high' and 'low',
I wished the night would stay the same...
it showed the 'glory' of Your name.

I will return another night....
to see, again, your mighty sights ~
and thank you, Lord, for giving me;
Creations of Your majesty.

Diane Ranker Riesen

God's Splendor

Photographer: Robert Gahris

God's Splendor

My soul leaps ever freely, boundless from each billowed
    cloud ~
And see abundant beauty gleam from visions down below-
A million words could not describe, if spoken clear out
    loud…
How perfect is God's splendor ~ in His proof I now could
    know.

Diane Ranker Riesen

God's Work

Photographer: Debra Hoffman Gardner

God's Work

Alone..out on the water ~ I feel your presence near;
I always sense you stronger…whenever I am here.
The ocean's mighty majesty; it's never-ending view ~
When I rest within it's glory… I stop and pray to You.

How Great your mighty power must be ~
what miracles You've made;
and as I stop and look around…..
so many are displayed.

This strong, engulfing water ~
all the 'life' that lives within…..
and all it's different memories ~
Where did it all begin?

When I'm alone and praying…
as the tide rolls gently past ~
I thank You for this glory;
so perfect, free, and vast.

Diane Ranker Riesen

Goodbye My Friend

Photographer: Ann & Ashley Bishop

Goodbye, My Friend

Goodbye, my friend, for just this while…
your sky-blue eyes and crazy smile.
Goodbye for now, but not the end…
We'll all join up ~ and smile again.

You made us laugh until we cried…
and all those times… will never die.
Our love-filled times are etched in stone;
with these… we'll NEVER be alone.

Goodbye, my young and crazy friend…
whose laughter never seemed to end;
Your sparkling eyes will light the night ~
and we will all enjoy the sight!

You hated sorrow, hurt, and pain….
so ~ we will look beyond this rain.
You taught us joy… and how to love ~
just keep on teaching… from above.

This moment's time is just a 'blink' ~~~
"Forever" lives in what we think.
And we will know you're here, my friend…
Until we all meet up again!

Diane Ranker Riesen

Grieve Not

I watch you wake to each new day, I see your silent tears ~
You think I'm gone and you're alone…
but, I am always near.
I can't explain in words you know~
what happens when you die;
I know you question why I'm gone…
I know you wonder "why".

If I could only show you in a way you'd really feel~~~~~
what happiness I have now, and prove that Heaven's real ~
Although you cannot see me ~ I'm
alive MORE than before.
My time on earth was wonderful….
but, Heaven's even more!

Within those silent moments… when
you wish I still was there…
I pray you sense the joy I feel ~ my soul is everywhere.
No matter what you're doing; no matter what you see---
whenever you feel softly calmed;
that love will be from 'me'.

Diane Ranker Riesen

Hamster's Wheel

Photographer: Mike Stevenson

Hamster's Wheel

Have you ever been caught in a huge, thick crowd,
Trying so hard to see?
You know there's so much more ahead…
But you're stuck in the midst of a sea.

You haven't the strength to forge on through
So you hold on to each sight you find.
You imagine how wondrous the view must be ~
You envision it deep in your mind.

Have you ever felt caught in a hamster's wheel?
Each struggle seems endless and long;
Yet, you keep up the journey; your body is weak ~
But your love and your spirit are strong.

There are those here in life who are born with a cause.
They cast 'heavenly' light on their way.
We don't know they are 'angels' who hide in disguise,
And bring gifts of great hope every day.

I was blessed to know one of these warriors of God,
who covered each pain with a smile.
God uses these angels to teach us 'pure love',
and the faith to walk through every trial.

This 'miracle angel' disguised as a child,
Who was able to stay just 'awhile' ~
changed each life she met with her soft, gentle soul -
and the sight of God's love in her smile.

Diane Ranker Riesen

Have We Done Well

Photographer: Diane Ranker Riesen

Have We Done Well?

Have we done well? ~ Lord, we've wondered..
Have we done all that we should?
Has she grown to be the woman....
that You always hoped she would?
From the moment that You sent her...
did You always have a 'plan'?
You need to know how blessed we feel.
We hope You understand.

A million other parents could have gotten her to raise;
but, You trusted our decisions; and our
choices through these days.
We've always known how fortunate;
and lucky that we were.....
of all the countless babies..... You entrusted us with her!

So much of who our daughter is...
she learned along the way.
We tried to set examples ~ by the way we lived each day.
Yet, still we often question...If we did all that we could;
the time has gone so quickly...
Did we do all that we should?

"My children, do not worry, do not dwell upon those fears;
I had chosen long before her birth that
'you' would help her years.
I knew before you got her...that you
were the ones she'd need;
To teach her all life's lessons, to love her, and to lead.

You both have made Me very proud..
to gaze upon her face;
I've never wanted anyone… to raise her, in your place.
She grew up with the kind of love ~
I planned for her to know..
You were chosen long before your births..
to help My Child to grow.

Her heart is full of tenderness, her
eyes are filled with light;
She shows the love you taught her; and
she's learned to do what's right.
She had a choice to make herself;
although you led the way…..
And she chose the path you taught
her; she amazes Me each day.

Delight in how you've raised her, she's
'your' child as well as Mine;
She's so special in a million ways…. with heavenly 'design'.
Her life is just beginning; she has all the love she'll need…
And with the Faith she clings to…
her "Forever's" guaranteed!"

Diane Ranker Riesen

HE

Photographer: Jim & Lynne Anthony

HE

Who says that Nature's all by chance?
Each Season came to be.
Why can't a great "Divinity"
be part of what we see?

Can all we know in this great world....
create a moonlit sky?
The universe is endless ~
And no one knows quite 'why'?

I don't believe in circumstance...
when I gaze upon a flower;
I don't believe each petal formed ~
without a higher 'power'.

And when I sit out in the wind...
and bathe myself in 'Sun' ~
I know without a moment's pause,
that "GOD" was how it's done.

Diane Ranker Riesen

He Answers

My soul is tired, wrought and worn,
I look for answers as I'm torn.
This life brings pain and spares no time—
I search for strength to comfort mine.
There seems to be no reason clear,
- so many suffer, ache, and die;
Yet, when my Faith starts wearing thin~
as earnestly I question why~~~~
a soft, sweet, gentle wave of peace
sweeps through my soul and makes me weep—
warm, tender tears of Godly grace…
And softly blessed… I fall asleep.

Diane Ranker Riesen

Hearts

Our hearts can hold a thousand different things ~
Old memories from the past and newer dreams...
I've felt it whisper, cry, ... and even Sing!
My heart is like a friend ~ it sometimes seems.

I wonder with each person passing by ~
what heavy burdens lay upon their way....
And yet, they still have strength to always try;
Their tender hearts must help them through each day.

This world can be so busy, fast, and loud;
But, in the silence ~ I hear my heart beat ~
That sign of life is silenced by the crowd.....
But, 'quiet' lets me hear it -- soft and sweet.

I wish that we could all just see inside.....
the beauty and the love inside each heart;
I think that if we all just really tried ~
we'd find our hearts aren't very far apart.

Diane Ranker Riesen

Heaven Stayed

Photographer: Toria Felton

Heaven Stayed

My soul was never empty...... I'm not sure 'how' I knew;
As far back as my mind goes.... I
always knew there's 'YOU'.
I've never had to wonder .. or search to find what's "real" ~
I knew that YOU existed ~ it's something I could "feel".

I guess that's why it's hard for me ~
to understand the search....
the yearning that so many feel... the emptiness and 'thirst'.
I'm not sure that it served me well ~
to never know that 'need'...
I never knew the 'searching'..and
where the quest would lead.

I guess some souls are sent to earth...
whose memories still are there ~
Of the glory that we come from ~
and we're totally aware ....
that Heaven really does exist and God is truly real ~ ~
and maybe I can show the 'Way'.. for
those who want to "feel"?

I've heard amazing journeys... told from
many souls who searched ~
I've watched them change from feeling 'lost'...
and those 'transformed' in church.
I'd hate to have to know one hour...
not knowing what is 'real'....
So I want to try to live my life and help the 'others' feel.

It really is 'quite easy'… it isn't hard to know ~
The truth of our existence dwells deep inside our soul.
Just ask "God" if He's really there,
just put aside your 'doubt'..
God will open up your heart, and show what life's about.

I know God wants each one of us…
He wants nobody "lost"….
It matters not how 'long' it takes ~ He'll try at any cost ~
He wants each of his children…. to
come back home one day;
How Great if we could help just 'one'……
to start them on their way!

Diane Ranker Riesen

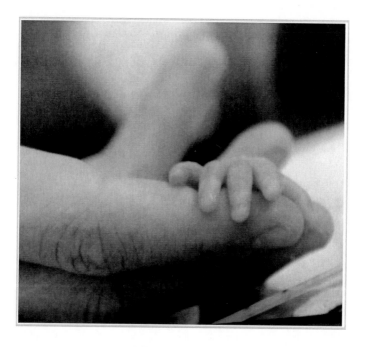

Heaven's Child

Photographer: Ashley Joliat Ardner

Heaven's Child

I've often wondered quietly ~~~ just
how God's home must feel;
Will I be truly happy? Will everything seem real?

They say there are no words to use...
to show the Joy you'll find ~
And yet, I've wished God could relay
a glimpse..inside my mind.

He heard and blessed me with a touch ~~
of what will follow 'death'..
He let's me see it's 'beauty' and 'feel' an angel's breath.

Each question that I've pondered, each
thought that burdened me ~
are answered in each baby's face ~ that miracle I see!

Diane Ranker Riesen

Heaven's Not So Far Away

There were so many thoughts I used to have…
Those things that I believed when I was small ~
My world was filled with simple joys and smiles;
I had no heavy worries, none at all.

But with each passing year I watched things change….
And saw that life can bring us certain pains;
I realized that there's no guarantee…..
with all the sun…. We'll also have some rain.

I lost someone I loved…. And then I knew ~
That this is just a 'life' we're passing through.
I knew deep down that this was not the 'end' ~
And I would see my loved one once again.

I prayed for God to give my soul some hope ~
I struggled for some 'Peace' that He might give..
And just when I was sure I couldn't cope ---
God showed me that our souls will always 'live'.

He showed me that our loved ones follow close,
and just when we are needing them the most ~~~
We'll see them all around us through the day--
Heaven's really not so far away.

That little breeze you'll feel across your hair---
is just a sweet reminder that they're there.
Each time you see the beauty of a smile --
is just more proof they're with you all the while.

Our fleeting time on earth is not the end ~
We all will see our loved ones once again.
Remember that until our meeting day....
Heaven's really not that far away.

Diane Ranker Riesen

He Hears You

Photographer: Lory Kobelt "The Icing"

He Hears You

You don't need to cry out loud…
You don't need to plea;
God lives deep inside of you—
and He lives inside of me.

You don't need to wonder…
if God can feel your pain;
He knows when your heart's shining—
And He knows when your heart rains.

There's no need to count your prayers…
He's heard you all along;
That 'strength' you have to make it through—
It's "GOD"… who made you strong.

A prayer is not reciting…
A prayer is not a chore;
It's just some time with you and Him—
It opens 'Heaven's door'.

When you seem lost and all alone…
'Be Still' and close your eyes;
reach down into your quiet soul—
You'll see 'hope' never dies.

Diane Ranker Riesen

Hello God

Photographer: Sharon Dundore Wadelin

Hello, God

A butterfly just landed on my knee;
as soon as I sat down ~ it greeted me.
I went outside to breathe in nature's 'air' ~
before I knew it... you were sitting there.

I don't think I had ever had the chance ~
most times I only saw a fleeting glance.
Now, as I sat just gazing at your wings...
I 'knew' that only God could make these things.

Each detail was a marvelous design!
Such beauty only comes from the 'Divine'.
And, oh the colors like a painting rare ~
my eyes were 'froze'... as you stay sitting there.

They say that only God can make a tree;
but, that sweet, tender moment made me see ~
that God's the great designer of it all...
and as I gazed around, I cried in 'awe'.

There cannot be another answer why ~
our world suspends beneath the perfect sky.
I knew that day that God is truly there...
He shows Himself in nature 'everywhere'!

Diane Ranker Riesen

Hidden Angels

I watch each person passing by ~
they're busy on their way;
so many things to finish, so much to fill their day.
But, just when I am saddened by the hectic rush of life-
a total stranger lifts my mood, amid the frenzied strife.
This stranger can be anyone... just casually passing by;
but takes the time to wink at me and say a simple "hi" ~
It's amazing how a tiny gesture changes any day...
from ordinary 'hidden angels' tossed along my way.

Diane Ranker Riesen

His Hope

Photographer: Sydni Claunch

His Hope

Dear God, I woke this morning with
such sorrows on my mind ~
it's times like this, ~ I wonder if there's any 'joy' to find.
I know this world is beautiful; I know
YOU want our trust……
but sometimes all the sorrows seem
to burden me so much.

I'm trying hard to understand through
all my doubtful thoughts~
and keep in mind the beauty, and the
'joys' that You have brought.
But, some days I am weaker - and I falter through the day;
My heart is burdened heavy with the
sorrows brought our way.

Yet, even in this darkness ~ You never seem to fail…..
You send me touches of Your love; so I can then prevail.
I pray for all the sadness; and I pray
You'll send some hope..
to help each worried loved one ~ and
give them strength to cope.

I trust you, Lord… though all this pain;
I know we'll make it through ~
whenever we are tired and weak;
we'll get our strength from YOU.

Diane Ranker Riesen

His Power

Artist: Leo Diamantopoulos

His Power

I saw a tiny flower....just struggling to break through ~
The soil was thick and very dry...
Yet, 'green' came into view.
What made this little flower ~~ work so hard to thrive...
to struggle through these issues; just to stay alive?

It would have been much easier..
for this young plant to die ~
yet, through those tough conditions....
that 'greenery' caught my eye.
I remember thinking 'nature' ... has
our same strong will to fight...
that flower never gave up.... to reach up to the light.

God gives us all some hidden power...
not always clearly known;
But, when we're struck with struggle...
our strength is always shown.
Just like this tiny flower... no matter hard or slow ~
Give yourself that inner strength..
and let God's power grow!

Diane Ranker Riesen

Hometown Then

Photographers: Cindy Shuff Peacock (top)
Bonnie Mack (bottom)

Hometown Then

(Tiffin, Ohio)

I walked the sidewalks long ago ~ in my
sweet hometown, once again;
I remember tender memories… though some
fifty years have passed since then.

When I was young, the times were
sweet~ as innocence was strong….
there was no fear to walk alone; as
rarely things went wrong.
I walked my way to school each morn;
and never feared the way ~
My hometown held security and I felt safe each way.

As children we would all head out….
to play out in the sun~
We'd jump our ropes, and ride our
bikes until the day was done.
Off to Oakley Park we'd head ~ to
climb among the trees…..
We'd use the bars, and swing so high ~
just playing in the breeze.

We'd bike our way down River Road…
our journey yet unknown ~
We always rode with others ~ but we weren't afraid 'alone'.
Times have changed since I was young;
and now new fears abound…
that simple freedom that I had ~ is no longer around.

As each year goes; I thank the days
when I was very young ~
The times seemed innocent and clear;
but, now that time is done.
When I get sorrowed by these times ~
I know I had the 'best'.
I think back on my childhood… and
know that I was 'blessed'.

I take a walk inside my mind ~ and
see those sight's again….
Hedges Park, and Jolly's … the stately 'Courthouse' then ~
I'm glad I grew up when I did ---
those young and simple days;
My hometown formed my character ~
a million different ways.

Diane Ranker Riesen

Adam

How Can Heaven Smile

In Memory of Adam Perna

How Can Heaven Smile?

I wonder, in my silent grief ~~ how Heaven still can smile -
to welcome back my precious child, I had for just a while?
So short a time I held him......... I long to see his face.
Yet, God's strong hand reached through the clouds; and
    took you from this place.
Can it be true?............... The Angels sang!
How dare there be such joy ~
My heart is torn, and I am lost ~
without my darling boy.
I've prayed for answers endlessly, in darkness, ~ on my knees,
I've asked the Lord to listen;... and hear my constant pleas.
             Then late, last night.... in stillness ~~~~
             When no one else was near,
        I kept my soul wide open, and listened 'hard' to hear.
"My child~   I'm never far away; your prayers, I've heard
    each one.
I KNOW your pain so clearly ~~ I, too, have lost a son."
"Sometimes a precious miracle, is taken from this earth –
And you'll not know till later ~ what your sacrifice was
    worth.
My plan is ever perfect... and one day you will see;
Your questions will be answered....   when you come home
    to ME."

                            Diane Ranker Riesen

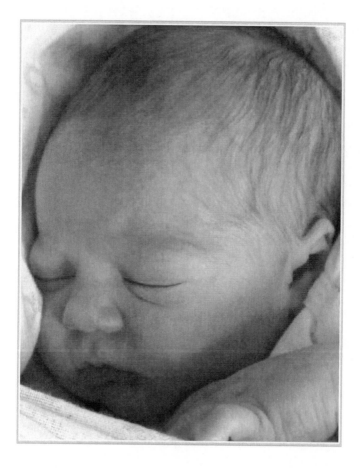

Infant Dream

Photographer: Kaitlyn Ranker Bishop

Infant Dream

(Brent 1983)

There has never been so clearly, such a vision ~ soft and
nearly
        — just as perfect as I'd prayed —
Yet, in one small, gentle infant ~ lay the magic in an
instant
        to beam miracles as he laid.

All the pain the world can offer, all the sorrows strong
around -
        Were concealed by looking at him;
        I was blessed by what I found.

Untainted yet by greed, pure and joyous as a light,
        ~ this sweet child held God's blessing ~
        all that makes our struggles right.

        - And, when, by chance, I may drift outward -
        ….off the path that I should take….
    ~~ I can stop… and 'dream' his beauty ~~
        Then be saved ~ when I awake.

                      Diane Ranker Riesen

I Thought

Photographer: Deb Ranker Kahler

I Thought

I thought I saw you, yesterday ~ around the corner, on my way...
>And yet I know this could not be... for Heaven's your reality.

Still, there are moments tossed in time; when I can feel you near ~
>Although I cannot see you.... I know that you are here.

It's strange how I can sense you.... There's nothing I can see;
>My soul can feel your presence ~ it's right in front of me.

These fleeting brief encounters.... are such to make me feel ~
>Earth's life is just a journey.......... Eternity is real.

I see you in a million ways, and know you're watching near.
>You're in the rose I picked today, and in the birds I hear.

A thousand falling raindrops... a million flakes of snow ~
>You dance upon the sunlight ~~ as the summer breezes flow.

You play upon the waters, as I watch out from the shore;
>And in my darkest hours - You seem to help me more.

It isn't easy waiting..... A soul can miss so much ~~~~
>Yet, I know you're still beside me..... I can feel your spirit's touch.

Diane Ranker Riesen

I Was There

Photographer: Mark Riesen

I Was There

(The Cross)

I was there Lord, I confess with shame..
as You walked Your final miles.
I watched them curse and spit on You..
I stood there all the while.
I hid behind the massive crowd, I
followed as You stepped…
Along the path to Calvary. I hid my face and wept.

I watched You stumble to Your knees,
as others laughed with scorn.
I saw Your face grow weary, Your body tired and worn.
What made You take this suffering?
How could You bear this pain?
As the crowds stood there and mocked
You.. You continued just the same.

I saw the nails the soldiers used, to bond You to that tree;
I could not bear to watch them, as
You took that pain for me.
I wished that I were stronger; and
had tried to stop the day;
But, I was weak and timid… there
was nothing I would say.

I saw You rise in torment, as they lifted up Your cross
So determined to bear every pain, and suffer any loss.
At one point, as I gazed above.. I think I caught Your eye..
What kind of love could keep You
there.. to suffer, then to die?

Your Father sent You years before…
a young babe born in straw;
To use Your love for sinners– and then to die for all.
How hard this journey must have been;
what torment You would face.
You deserved the kindness due a King,
yet suffered in our place.

I've tried to fathom such a love; the
kind that bears no cost…
A love that's undeserving and will suffer any loss.
I never asked for this Great Love;
nor earned my soul set 'free';
Despite my undeserving… You gave Your death for me.

Diane Ranker Riesen

I Wish

Some people look right at me... and only see my 'face' ~
while other's look right through me.....
and just see 'empty' space.
I wish there was a way for us.... to
see right to the 'heart'....
I think we all would realize... we're not that far apart.

We all look different 'physically' ~
by no means of our own;
A million different factors shape the
way we're built and grown.
I wish I knew when I was young...
the things that I know now ~
that even all the greatest 'minds'....
are still just learning 'how'.

I always thought I had to be 'exactly' like the rest ~
I couldn't be the normal me.......I had to be the best.
I would have been much happier ~
to just be simply 'me'....
My worries would be 'lifted'... and
my burdens be set 'free'.

I wish the world was simpler; there's
just too much going by ~
There's so much pain and sorrow....
and I just can't figure 'why'?
No one's 'better' than the rest..... no
soul deserves 'more' care...
I wish we all were equal ~ any judgement isn't fair.

I think we all can change this world ~
I think we really can;
if we just work together... and learn to understand ~
that we are "each" a worthy soul...
and each of us could 'see';
that all of us belong here... that we are 'family'.

Diane Ranker Riesen

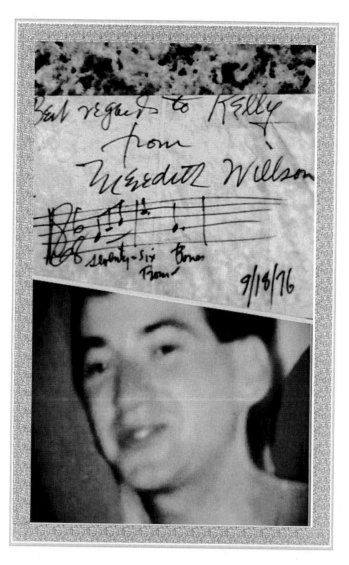

If A Soul Could Sing

Photographer: Kelly Addis

If a Soul could Sing

My soul contains a million songs
And yet, I find no way;
To let the music play aloud…
And tell what I must say.

So many dreams and thoughts are lost;
Within my silent space-
I search to find the means to show~
The gifts inside that place.

My soul withholds each miracle;
I witness every day.
I wish a song could burst within—
To sing what I must say.

There are no words that can express
The secrets of my soul;
Each smile, each countless dream come true;
Has made my spirit whole.

I cannot give my melody…..
It seems it's mine to keep.
Each one must search their quiet place;
~ and find their song down deep.

Diane Ranker Riesen

If I Could

Photographer: Pamela D. R. Bibler

If I Could

If I were with you, here and now ~
and I could talk to you somehow.....
I'm not sure I'd know what to say;
and how my love's grown every day.

I hoped that if I were to leave..
If God had plans ~ and you would grieve;
That somehow all my love would stay..
and help you make it through your way.

To my surprise and great relief ~
the love we had has slowed your grief..
Death cannot steal what we have shared-
Where once was fear ~ I am NOT scared.

You've taken all the love inside -
Your heart is strong, and opened wide…
To use that strength and carry on~
and do what I depended on!

You've taken all that love we shared..
and shown it to the ones who care.
Our babies are not left alone-
I worried once ~ but, should have known.

God gives the strength for you to do…
all the things I hoped for you;
I haven't lost a single thing ~
I still have you ~ and EVERYTHING.

So, take your days, still left to give -
And honor me by how you live.
I'm watching, loving, knowing, still…..
'Forever's Ours' ~ I've seen God's will!

Diane Ranker Riesen

I'm Here

I'm here… right here… beside you; I'm everywhere you go.
I'm part of every breath you take ~
and deep inside your soul.
I'm closer now than ever ….. although you may not see.
Each day, each hour, each moment ~
Is spent along with me.

It's strange ~ I never thought that
I'd feel closer than before.
Your earthly eyes can't see me ~ yet I
watch through Heaven's door.
It's even better- where I'm at ~ Just
'believe' God knows what's best.
And when you get to where I am…
You'll understand the rest!

Don't let your 'earthly' understanding…
Take your joy away ~
My greatest joy and fondest wish is
that you *love* each day.
I'm happier than ever~~~ when I can see your smile!!!!!
The touch and talking that you miss
is gone for just awhile.

I have it all… I've never left.. We'll never be apart ~
I stand beside you always… and stay within your heart.
I used to wonder how it'd be ~ I wish each of you knew ~
Heaven makes things perfect ~ my
dreams have all come true.

Diane Ranker Riesen

In My Dream

Photographers: Luke & Sara Riesen

In My Dream

In my dream my soul was flying…and I looked down on
our 'earth',
I saw the world through God's view ~ and all that it is
worth ~
There was no damage done by man; no loss or pain
in view…..
I saw the world the way it looked…. when God had make it
new.

I wish it could have stayed that way… I was inspired by
awe -
The land was so untainted ~ and the mountains strong and
raw;
Each sight I saw was perfect; each stream was clear as
glass ~
The skies were filled with clarity…. the oceans blue and vast.

My dream was over quickly…. and then I realized ~
that this is how God sees "us" ~ we're PERFECT in His
eyes.
I'm going to try much harder to be the one HE sees;
I want Him smiling softly; and make HIM proud of me.

Diane Ranker Riesen

In My Room

Did you hear Me when you woke?
I sent a sweet 'hello'….
My voice was not the way you planned;
I was ~ that bird ~ you know.

Your curtain rustled softly….
as a silent breeze slipped through.
I was seeking your attention -
and was 'whispering' to you.

I dance upon your pillow,
and peek into your dreams….
My moonlight casts soft shadows
as, across your room, it streams.

Sit with Me, in darkness ~
My stars will light the night.
My arms will reach around you soft…
as We behold the sight.

For all the wonders ~ past your room…
The sky and trees, you see;
All that nature offers…
are secret gifts from Me.

Don't ponder when you'll see Me,
or whether far, or near ~
Just closely look around you….
You'll see I'm always here.

Diane Ranker Riesen

Just Pray

Photographer: Brenda Windau Pisani

Just Pray

When life is overwhelming ~ and sadness grabs our day;
when all the sun's light disappears;
behind clouds dark and gray ~
It may seem so much easier... to let
pain steal your smile....
but there is something stronger that you should do awhile.

Just sit down somewhere quiet ~
and close your eyes to pray;
Those private, sacred moments... will redirect your day.
Prayer is nothing tangible; and so it often feels....
that you should be more active ~ but,
prayer is much more real.

The power that is transferred... into
your soul from 'high' ~
will give you all the strength you
need... and help you to get by.
Your soul is touched by God's own hand;
He makes you very strong ~
Despite your doubts and worry ~ you're shielded all along.

Praying is a precious gift ~ a perfect, magic power.....
that calms your fears, and lifts you....
out of your darkest hour.
God sits and waits to hear from you ~
He loves to share each day...
Your prayers will be your comfort;
and protect you on your way.

Diane Ranker Riesen

Last Night

Last night, as I lay sleeping sound……
I woke ~ and saw some 'light' around;
I sensed another soul took flight~
another angel flew last night.

How beautiful; the moment when….
I feel that joy of peace again;
How glorious the time must be ~
when someone's soul is finally free!

I feel such comfort knowing then;
another Angel flies again ~
I pray to join them all one day…
as 'Heaven-bound' .. I'm on my way!

Diane Ranker Riesen

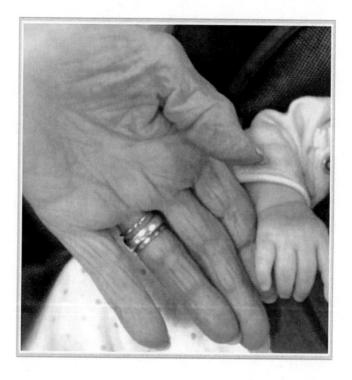

Life Cycle

Photographer: Jeanne Vera Ardner

Life Cycle

When I'm alone and take the time....
to pause and think of years gone past;
I search through countless memories..
And see how youth has faded fast.

The years tell me I'm older now ---
Each year ~ so much has changed.
Just when I think I'm settled ~
My life is rearranged.

I think of couples starting out....
I think back on my past ~
The diapers, toys, and meetings;
And how they end so fast.

I was that carefree child...once;
I was so new and young....
But, now MY Children take that place ~
Life's "cycle" had begun.

I see myself in 'them' now ~
As they walk the paths so worn.
And when 'they' reach the walkway's end....
NEW children will be born.

Just as our parents watched us....
and we watched 'ours' the same;
Life's 'cycle' will continue...
as new children join the game.

We're here for such a fleeting time ~
Take pause along the way....
To notice all God's miracles --
And cherish EVERY day!

Diane Ranker Riesen

Living the Tradition

Photographer: Dan Kontak

Living the Tradition

(Tiffin Columbian High)

The young boys dressed out on the field;
to learn the magic told ~ Of all the men who
played the game ~ from very new to old;
the football teams that practiced hard;
regarding each condition ~ had dreams to be a
part of what was known.... as the 'tradition'.

Each different team all dressed as one --
all born to love the game;
to touch the ball, to run the field,
with little thought of 'fame' ~
would train and work through high school days....
to follow each rendition....
And be a part of what was called ....
"The TORNADO tradition!"

Those youthful years of football hours,
the sacrifice and pain ~ were worth the sweat and
challenge.. for the lessons that were gained.

They say there is no equal game; that 'magic'
of a team ~ that struggles through each trial
and fight.. to try to reach a dream.

You pushed your limits to the end ~
and proved you had the stuff...
to play the game and run the field;
through smooth times and in rough.

And, as you neared that dream you had;
to own that great 'tradition'.......a turn of fate,
so near your goal, will damage your condition.

You had a 'taste' of Friday's thrills ~ to win at any cost......
but, now the lights, the crowds and cheers..
will bring a sense of 'loss'.

Your once strong muscles, lean and fit ~
are torn by life's unyielding hit;
and you must stay to only 'watch' ~~
be silenced and to yield ~
while all your teammates live their dreams ~~
out there on the field.

And yet, your strength still shines so bright ~
you cheer your team with pride;
and though you could not 'play' the game...
your victory never died.

You showed the real strength of a man ~
knocked to the ground; but, still to stand ~
A heart of gold and 'will' of stone....
to 'walk the walk' ..then sit alone.

It serves no use to wonder 'why'; or question turns of life ~
Your days will always have some joy…
and also, times of strife.
But "football" games are only won
by each part of the team ~
and you were right there with them…
a strong part of their 'dream'!

All through your life, tough times occur ~
in many hard conditions…
But, you will use your lessons learned;
by living the "tradition"!

Diane Ranker Riesen

Lost Angels

Photographer: Diane Ranker Riesen

Lost Angels

(In tribute to Anna's 5 angels)

There are such times that stop our hearts;
and cause our breath to slow.....
those moments so unbearable; our
fragile minds can't know.
In those deep, endless days of dark ~
attempts to help will fail ~
no earthly love can ease the pain… no comfort can prevail.

What can we do to carry on? What answer can there be?
There seems to be no solace; and no way to set us free.
A numbness creeps into our souls ~
no distant signs of hope;
We pray God understands us…. and
the way we need to cope.

For no more shall a single tear stream
down our swollen cheeks ~
We shall stand firm and let no pain
of sadness make us weak!
No tortured anguish, tear-filled eyes,…
we shall not show our grief;
For nothing can sustain us ~ or give us some relief.

And then we pause, and close our eyes;
and KNOW our loss is real ~
Would it be best to close our hearts,
and pretend we didn't feel?
God knows the truth is in between ~
the numbness and the screams;
We can't ignore the loss we feel…
and all our broken dreams.

We must take time for sorrow ~ we
must take time to feel….
for we have lost some miracles; and only time will heal.
The greater that our love was ~ the worse our loss will be~
Our God lost His child also; and His love will set us free.

Diane Ranker Riesen

Lost Prayer

When I can find no prayers to pray ~
and sorrow steals my way;
I feel my soul is empty and I have no words to say ~
I lay my head and close my eyes… and
know that YOU are there…..
You understand my weakness and the burden that I bear.

I know my God sees everything; and
that He knows my heart ~
He knows that I feel helpless… and
don't know where to start.
It is those times of 'empty'… when
I know God intercedes….
He takes my silence gently; and gives me what I need.

I never need to wonder… if my prayer is strong enough ~
God doesn't mind my weakness --
He just embraces 'Love',
and then I can lay quietly and know
my prayers were heard…..
God took each one to handle ~ without a single 'word'.

Our "feelings" can be prayer, too ~
He needs no voice from you…..
Just raise your needs to Heaven;
God will see you through.

Diane Ranker Riesen

Maya Angelou

(May 28, 2014)

Through your sweet soul came words of hope,
such perfect written flowing streams…
of wondrous glories in our world~
and unseen wishes in our dreams.

And, Oh.. what peace your voice would sing -
of glories seen and kindness shown….
Your words will echo endlessly -
and shine in places yet unknown.

Your gift of life was meant to bring ~
such priceless lessons weaved by hand;
Your words gave comfort to the lost ~
and helped our world to understand.

Fly high now ~ where the angels dance ~
and claim the joys your praise would show;
Your shining light has dimmed for now..
but through your words… your life will grow.

Diane Ranker Riesen

Missing You

Sometimes there are no words to show
what lies within your heart ~
Sometimes a million prayers can't lift
the hurt when love departs.....
But, when a "true" love's time is past,
and you are left alone;
You feel your loved one closely by ~
in ways that can't be known.

A million scattered memories, a thousand different ways~
your loved one speaks so clearly to you each and every day.
We never really die, you see, we're never really far ~
You'll see me in each blade of grass..
and every shining star.

Diane Ranker Riesen

My Father's Gift

Photographer: Nadine Felton

My Father's Gift

My Father knew that in the end,
when human souls had all been spent;
A higher strength is what they'd need,
to clear their hearts and then repent.
He knew your sins were far too strong
and even though you felt sincere~
No earthly power could save your life ~
and so He chose to send 'ME' here.

I felt the struggles life would bring,
and knew great pain along my way-
But all along, I trusted God;
and that is why 'I' chose to stay.
So many times I felt alone,
no one could know the weight I bore;
My Father stayed right by My side…
I knew I couldn't ask for more.

The time arrived as God had planned —
for ME to save My fellow man –
I knew that I'd endure the task,
the miracle of God's pure plan.
I felt the hurt of hatred ~ and I suffered horribly;
But knew My God was with Me as I died upon that tree.

My Father paved the way for you, He made salvation clear.
His Spirit longs to be with you ~
there's nothing you should fear.
My human body tortured, as I died upon that Cross –
My Father offered up His son…
YOUR soul was worth the loss.

Diane Ranker Riesen

My Friend

Photographer: Braden & Jace Riesen

My Friend

I lost my best friend yesterday....
my best friend from the start ~
I used to share my feelings and the secrets in my heart.
I never had to wonder if he loved me... or he cared.....
each time that I felt lonely, my friend was always there.

When I knew that he was really gone,
I ran outside to pray ~
I wanted God to show me that I'd see my friend one day.
I didn't know what I should say..
or know the words to share...
"Would I see my dog in Heaven?
Will all our pets be there?

Then, as I sat there quietly.... I looked up to the sky ~
I asked God why the ones I love ~ always have to die.
I don't know how to tell you...I just felt it in my 'heart'...
God let me know that none of us will ever be apart.

I knew without a single doubt~
that 'he' would wait for me;
and when I get to Heaven; he'll be the first I see!
God said He'll make it perfect...
and we never 'really' die.....
I knew I'd see my dog again ~ I didn't say 'Good bye'.

Diane Ranker Riesen

My Prayer

Photographer: Glenn & Paula Burgderfer

My Prayer

Dear Lord, I have a prayer tonight ~
this one is just for me;
I need your power to change myself
and be "who" I should be.
I know you see the best in us…..
and "I" have so much more…
to offer other people ~ and do what I'm 'here' for.

There's not a single movement…
or a breath that I could take;
Without your mighty power ~
I would simply fall and break.
And so, tonight, I offer 'YOU'.. my entire heart and soul ~
to fix what I need mended ~ and make my spirit whole.

Diane Ranker Riesen

My Tree

Artist: Miranda Ranker

My Tree

To stand beneath your outspread arms…
in sheltered safety from the wind;
or lie back on the cooling grass, and
look up through your leaves –
I dream of all the lives you've shared,
the times you've seen expire;
and know your soul rejoices, and know your spirit grieves.

God's great creation standing tall… amidst a million more,
Your roots grow deep in memories,
with stories gone untold.
But, think upon your majesty and all that you have seen ~
Countless dreams of youthful minds..
release as leaves unfold.

How perfect can a tree's life be?
How peaceful, yet so strong ~
I lay beneath your safety,
And feel like I belong.

A hundred days will pass beyond…
when I am long and gone;
but you will hold my memories – within your quiet soul.
Amidst the raging winds and storms…
that follow through your days ~
All these moments – stilled in time …
will keep your spirit full.

Diane Ranker Riesen

My Walk

I walked along a simple path ~ the day was warm and
   clear…
I heard some soothing water from a brook that followed
   near;
and all the tiny whispers from the birds up in the trees ~
composed a masterpiece of love that played and sang for me.

That Oak tree in the distance ~ made me feel so very small….
I wondered of it's memories.. so stately, strong, and tall.
It's leaves were softly rustling as the wind came strolling
   through ~
I felt a sense of marvel with each touch of 'air' that blew.

And, Oh the joy I felt within…. as butterflies flew past;
with all the countless shadows that the sunshine caused to
   cast~
My own sweet private wonderland ~ my place away from
   home…
Where all God's perfect artwork was displayed for me ~ and
   shown.

Far back beyond some heavy brush… a movement caught
   my view ~
and as I strained to focus ~~~ a baby deer came through;
This hidden world of wonder, where God's miracles
   abound…
I saw His perfect handiwork in everything around.

My walk was almost finished …. but I didn't want to leave;
It showed me proof of all the hopes I wanted to believe ~
Yet, I can't stay forever ~ in all it's clarity.........
But, when I need assurance… I know it's there for me.

Diane Ranker Riesen

New Again

Photographer: Nadine Felton

New Again

Sometimes I wish I wasn't 'me' ~
and I could turn into a tree;
so stately as it firmly stands.. so simply, yet so truly grand!

I'd see the world through different eyes;
and bathe beneath the sky..
I'd take the time to closely watch ~ the seasons passing by.

In Summer, I am flourishing ~ with
all my branches dressed;
with countless leaves of different hues....
where butterflies can rest.

And then, with Fall... my leaves grow
dry; and slowly start to drop ~
I try to hold on to a few ~ but nothing makes them stop.

Then, oh so soon, the Winter looms ~
my roots prepare for cold;
I wonder just how strong I'll be...
as years keep growing old.

But, just when I am tired and worn ~
the Spring reveals it's face...
and where my bare, tired branches were...
new leaves will take their place.

Diane Ranker Riesen

No More Dreams

I think I saw a miracle…. alive and walking free ~
My heart wants to believe it's true; but, it can't really 'be';
Yet, at the time, it seemed so real…
and I could see your 'smile' -
and then I woke and knew that I had
dreamed it all the while.

I tried so hard to sleep again; I tossed
and turned and cried…..
for that one precious moment ~ I felt you hadn't died.
That tiny taste of Heaven… dissolved into the air ~
I had to sense all over….that you were never there.

Why do we lose the ones we love and have to carry on?
Why do we have to struggle ~ when you're already gone?
I guess the answer lies somewhere..
between our hearts and soul;
We feel the pain so strongly now ~
but, one day we will 'know'.

Time on earth is measured by each minute… every hour;
But those in Heaven live within a very different power.
They don't feel loss or sorrow ~ there
is no pain up there….
They get to keep the love they felt
and feel us "everywhere".

And so, till then, I'll really try ~
To live by Faith.. and not ask "Why?"
I'll strive to look where God is 'seen'....
until ~ I never have to dream.

Diane Ranker Riesen

Only God

Photographer: Maria Wahl

Only God

You and I can make a
wish…
dream a dream ~
enjoy a kiss.

We can think, create, and see…
but only GOD
can make a tree.

Diane Ranker Riesen

Peaceful Prayer

Photographer: Miranda Ranker

Peaceful Prayer

I walked among the trees today ~ to
gather up my thoughts…..
My life can swallow so much time
… my feelings just get lost.
I forget why I am really here; and what life's all about ~
I never want to lose the truth ~ I never want to doubt…
that God is why we're living; that He gave us our days -
and so, I go out in the woods ~ to take some time to pray.

"Dear God, don't ever let me lose the purpose I am here ~
Give me courage ~ and Your strength, to conquer any fear.
Please give my heart the power… to feel what You desire;
so that I not grow weary ~ that my purpose never tire.

The world's so large and I'm so small ~
I fear I can't do much…
Please.. when I feel defeated ~ I pray to sense Your touch.
You've told me every time I'm here …
that You will lead me through ~
and with that reassurance ~ my soul will follow YOU".

Diane Ranker Riesen

Prayer

Photographer: Jeanne Vera Ardner

Prayer

I used to think that praying was a necessary chore ~
and when I finished with the words; I felt I needed more.
I memorized the thoughts I prayed..and said them every
   night…
but, somehow, even with this time ~ 'something' wasn't right.

One night, as I was praying~ all the same, familiar words…
My mind got very quiet; and this is what I heard ~ ~ ~

"Why do you try so deeply ~ to prepare each thing you pray?
Why do you practice and rehearse the things you want to
   say?
I'm right here with you, listening… and want to hear your
   heart ~
I want to merely 'be' with you, and never feel apart.
Your prayers should just be simple ~ and what you really feel;
No practice is expected…. I want your feelings 'real'."

Right then and there, I realized ~ how precious prayers can
   be;
God doesn't want just mindful thoughts.. He wants some
   'time' with me!
I never wait till night now ~ I send thoughts through the
   day….
God took that special time with me ~ and showed me how
   to pray!

Diane Ranker Riesen

Quiet

I love a day that 'whispers'..
that never gets too 'loud' ~
I love to lay back on the grass-
and marvel at a cloud.

I don't mind all the 'quiet'…
it gives me time to 'pray' ~
I don't get tired of listening….
"HE" has so much to say.

Diane Ranker Riesen

Remember

Photographer: Melanie Edris

Remember

There is no greater joy around…….
nor sweeter moments to be found;
than all the times you've shared with friends ~
A memory made… that never ends.

We seem to take for granted ..
all the ordinary days ~
when "life" just seems to happen —
with no trials in the way.

We always seem to concentrate
on times that cause us pain.
We seem to overlook the sun ~
and stay long.. in the rain.

We need to take a moment…
even when our day is fast ~
…to make note of the simple things;
the happiness that lasts.

I need to take my own advice..
I need to hear it clear.
"Don't miss the beauty all around;
and the love that's always here".

Diane Ranker Riesen

Sherman

Photographer: Diane Ranker Riesen

Sherman

I knew I needed something… I felt so all alone;
I had more love to offer ~ and my children were all grown.
I think God heard my simple dream..
and thought He'd show a 'way',
"His" magic started working - I brought
"Sherman" home that day.

This tiny, little bundle ~ barely big enough to hold;
a soft and precious piece of love so tender to behold ~
It barely took a second for my heart to start to melt…
a complete and perfect love ~ was exactly what I felt.

It doesn't take a huge amount to fill an empty soul ~
We all just need someone to love..
to help our life feel whole.
It's not the things he does for me ~
it's "joy" that he conveys….
a pure and gentle tenderness surrounds him where he lay.

I'm not sure how I found him on that solitary day ~
It seemed to happen instantly ~ once I began to pray.
I do know that God sent him… especially for me -
and so much of my loneliness was suddenly set free!

Diane Ranker Riesen

Shine Bright

One night I sat out all alone ~ and gazed up at the sky…
I felt the need to spend some time and open up my heart;
On this one, quiet evening ~ ~ I really don't know 'why' ~
but special little miracles… began right from the start.

I thought the dark would scare me….
there was no one in sight ~
But, I felt a special calmness;
alone there, in the night.

Those tiny little night sounds seemed
to sing a song so sweet ~
the blackness of the air just seemed
to blanket me with peace.
For some strange, special reason, my soul felt so complete;
and the comfort I was feeling.. just never seemed to cease.

About an hour later.. I looked up at the stars…..
the clearness of the night sky showed
me many~ near and far.
Those tiny twinkling points of light
just seemed to speak to me ~
and I could hear some quiet whispers ~ speak so tenderly.

"We're all here… everyone of us ~
that you have lost so far….
We linger all around you and we watch you from each star.
Don't ever think we've left you; we're here just like 'before',
I know it's hard to comprehend~ but,
we're really with you 'more'."

DIANE RANKER RIESEN

A truth of love came over me ...
and I felt touched by grace;
God let me know my loved ones...
have never left this place.
Now every time I see a star; just floating in the sky ~
I feel a secret happiness.... there's really NO goodbye.

Diane Ranker Riesen

Silence

Photographer: Maria Wahl

Silence

When my brain gets so congested,
with the noise that's 'everywhere'...
I put my hands together ~
And I close my eyes in prayer.

Don't let the countless voices...
continue and increase ~
Give yourself some silence...
to ease your sense of peace.

Diane Ranker Riesen

Soar

Artist: Christine Vera Mundschau

Soar

I soared upon your feathered wings ~
and flew among the clouds;
I let my troubles drift away.. and sang a song out loud.
I left my worries on the ground; and
stole this time for 'me'~
I'd forgotten how to just let go ~ How peaceful it could be!

I only thought of good things…. and the love I felt inside~
Renewing all my senses on this soft and perfect ride.
I saw my world in clarity; without the frenzied pace….
and I could finally feel my world …
was such a better place.

I have to always take the time to step back, and renew ~
the peaceful feelings in my soul; and keep my spirit new.
Sometimes I let the busy things
crowd out my joy each day..
But this perfect ride..inside my mind…
has shown my heart the way.

No longer will I let the hours of busy life destroy -
the magic waiting through each day ~
each simple, tender joy.
I'll close my eyes and steal away…
upon those feathered wings;
and stay among the clouds once
more ~ until my spirit sings!

Diane Ranker Riesen

Something Gone

Photographer: Diane Ranker Riesen

Something Gone

A piece of you just disappears…..
when both your parents die ~
It's not the way you loved them; or
the countless tears you cry.
It's just that soft awareness that you never were alone….
that bond of sacred union you had
shared; as you had grown.

I felt like I was drifting… all alone ~ somewhere in space;
I knew I still belonged here.. but I felt so out of place.
My life would never be exactly how I dreamed it'd be….
For now I had to move on- without them here with me.

The feeling never changes…. I've never been the same ~
I want to make them proud of me….
and carry on their name.
But, part of me is missing ~ it's 'nothing' you can see….
But when my parents left this world….
they took a 'part' of me.

I know I'll get it back one day… I
know that day will come ~
when everything I once was ~ will once again become.
Until that great reunion, there's a loss within my soul…..
but, when I get to Heaven ~ I will once again be 'whole'.

Diane Ranker Riesen

Still Here

I saw a shooting star last night;
I thought that it was you.
A moonbeam danced out on the lawn;
I knew you saw it, too.

Sometimes I feel a gentle breeze
brush softly through my hair ~
And when those moments happen…
I know that you are there.

Some days I take an early walk
and breath the morning air…
I watch the birds, the flowers, and sky ~
I see 'you' everywhere.

Our lives are very brief here….
there's so much more I'll see;
When it's my time to be 'there' ~
I know you'll be with me!

Diane Ranker Riesen

Strength

Photographer: Maria Wahl

Strength

Is it FAITH that keeps you peaceful;
is it love that keeps you strong ~
together with the inner strength you've carried all along?
I look at you and wonder ~ I can sense your joys ahead….
You'll be blessed beyond all measure…
when you finally leave this bed.

You've said sometimes you wonder…
if you've really DONE enough?
I smile at your sweet, tiny frame ~
so small and yet so tough;
You've taken every challenge that
The Lord has brought you to….
And you passed each day with honor while
God used HIS strength through you!

You amaze me, and you've taught me ~
in a million different ways…
about the most important things; and how to live each day.
Despite the many joyous years, the love, and all the fun ~
Your "Faith" will soon reward you…..
the best is yet to come!

Diane Ranker Riesen

Sweet Slumber

There you sleep so sweetly… and I'm
captured so completely ~
How can one so small and tender;
make all my heart surrender?

A Parent's Love

Each night while you are resting…
time is frozen as I stare ~
How can one such tiny infant steal
my heart just being there?

A Parent's Love

Sometimes I cry just watching you…
It comes up from my soul~
And I wonder if you feel me ~ I wonder if you know….

A Parent's Love

I'd move the world and stars for you…
and never once regret~
I hope this feeling never ends - I pray I won't forget…

A Parent's Love

If I should die tomorrow.... Every
dream I wished came true~
And every hope I prayed for ~ was
there, right there - in 'you'.

Diane Ranker Riesen

Sweetness

Photographer: Kelly (Jordan) Fuller

Sweetness

I've never seen in one small child ~
the kind of 'joy' I see...
A spirit filled with Happiness --
that always blesses 'me'!

I've never watched 'eyes' twinkle...
exactly like yours do ~
I've never heard a giggle;
that blesses through and through.

You seem to be so happy ~
It's a 'magic' way to be....
Every time I see you ~
I become a better "me"!

Diane Ranker Riesen

That Night

He walked the night, in humble trust;
this man of quiet 'grace'…
to find the spot his soul would sense ~
contained that special place.
A wintry, cold and blustering breeze
would follow as he searched…
A wife with 'child', who rode behind ~
upon a donkey perched.

His young wife holding firmly…. to
a love no one could part;
So many questions left untouched,
she trusted with her heart.
I can't imagine such a sight….in stoic pace they kept…..
with only 'faith' to lead their way, and
'hope' to guard their step.

This was no ordinary night, this was no simple search ~
He held the task to find a place of rare and simple worth.
Throughout the skies that star-filled
night would brightly lead the way;
Not to a room of splendor; but, to a barn of hay.

So many miles of walking ~ no rooms in any Inn…..
He saw the spot, his unborn child…..
would soon be sheltered in.
This meager barn made just of wood,
his heart was split and torn ~
Was not the place that he had hoped
his young child would be born.

DIANE RANKER RIESEN

This unknown throne of merely straw,
this barn with chill-filled space,
Was not what he had hoped for...... this ordinary place.
Yet, glory filled the rustic walls, and beauty filled the air ~
When the miracle of birth took place;
and the babe was laying there.

It would take some years to understand,
so many prayers and thought,
to really know the blessing ~ of what
that cold 'eve brought.
But, now we know it was the spot,
that comforted the "One".
The skies stood still, the heavens peeked;
and "God" adored His Son.

Our "God" had always known that we
would need help 'every' day;
..that we could never conquer the temptations in our way;
And so, to save our earthly sins ~ He
knew we'd need 'someone'....
He gave His greatest gift of all...... He sent His only Son.

Diane Ranker Riesen

The Depths

Photographer: Jeanne Vera Ardner

The Depths

Lift me, Lord, I'm falling deep ~ Give me strength before
I weep;
so much pain surrounds my heart..... I feel like I could
break a part.
There's so much sorrow everywhere and life can be so
mean ~
Evil lurks to strike us down - it's hidden and unseen.

All my loved ones struggle; and I don't know what to do ~
In these weakest moments ~ I plead for strength from You.
Give me words to comfort.... Give me love to share;
How can I protect them; and show them that I care?

In these dark, deep, lonely times ~ I lay down at your knees;
and pray your mighty power will encompass all their pleas.
My heart beats strong for those I love... I ache to see their
pain -
It's times like this I realize...why Christ was born and came.

We are not strong enough alone ~ our hearts will break so
fast;
we need Your mighty power... for the chance our souls will
last.
Shower all of us, Lord ~ please pour down rains of love.....
We cannot find our peace down here ~ please send it from
'above'.

Diane Ranker Riesen

The Struggle

There was a day not long ago ~ when
I thought 'all' was lost...
I couldn't see much happiness; no light at any cost.
And though my Faith is firm and strong...
my soul was broken down;
it seemed no matter how I tried ~
no solace could be found.

It's really not 'too' often.. when I feel so sad and broke;
I'd go to sleep in sorrow ~ not caring if I woke.
I think these moments happen.... to everyone some days;
this world can break our spirits in a million different ways.

It's at these troubled moments... that
I close my eyes to pray ~
I trust that God can understand the
thoughts I want to say.
And even though I still feel lost; I try to understand....
that only God can see what's real;
and it's not known to 'man'.

I feel ashamed that with my 'Faith'...
this world can shake me down;
I searched God's Word to understand ~
and 'this' is what I found-
Even Jesus questioned God as He hung from that tree ~
He was partly 'human' and struggled just like me.

Diane Ranker Riesen

The Years

My life is one continual chain of years ~
and each, more complex than the last...
leaves scants of precious memories
to my past.

I used to fear my years ~ and ward them off
as if they were a threat..
... and never let ~~
Another added wrinkle to my face.

But, somehow wrinkles still appeared.

My youth, so distant in my past ~
and yet, still clear...
was like a dream.

The innocence of my youth was useful then...
I was a child, so why pretend ~
I did not cherish every moment?

But, I grew old as everyone must do;
still clinging to those visions left in view.
More wrinkles came.

Each added year presented me my prime ..
Now here ~ all life brought burdens to my mind.
And each and every pain, I realize ~
was then a needed stage...to make me wise.

For this I loved my adding years.

Still resisting all the way…more wrinkles came ~
Which bring me to my present stage in life…
Now, I am old.

Thinking back upon my life, I see ~
that every year held special parts of me…
and I would not trade neither youth nor prime; when….
given a chance to start my life again.

Some old men sit and weep about their past….
because each year, from first until the last ~
was not completed as they wished.

I have the answer.

Each dawn before you start another day..
convince yourself to spend it in a way ~
to help yourself and all.

If every year is spent in righteous light…
and we remain ourselves from day to night ~
then as we grow much older…as is fate;
We'll never have regret or merely 'wait' -
for death.

And as I do, we'll sit back and contend ~
that we lived well, and need not to defend…
a single action in our lives.

And then, with all our wrinkles and old age....
We'll LOVE ourselves.

Diane Ranker Riesen

There's Joy

I thank God for those special days ~
when life just seems 'SO RIGHT'.
So many days are tougher....
and I need to really 'fight'.

But just when I am tired ~
and those special times seem gone;
I see a little 'miracle',
and realize I was wrong.

I saw that little baby -
just sleeping like a dream....
His precious face seemed glowing ~
like a light from Heaven's beam.

I walked outside and took a walk,
and there, before my eyes ~
a tiny bird took it's first flight....
as I was strolling by.

I felt a stirring in my soul...
and I soon realized ~
that I just need to really 'look',
there's "joy" before my eyes.

Diane Ranker Riesen

This Morning

My eyes awoke this morning…
with a sense of urgent need ~
I felt someone was hurting; and I had the need to plead.
I didn't know the reason or what
words that I should say …
But, I knew someone was needing help ~
so I began to pray.

"Dear Lord, this world can be so hard;
so many souls are weak ~
I pray that You will help them all.
I'll let my feelings 'speak',
Please take Your children one by one…
and hold them tight and near."
…and then I felt a touch of peace and
knew that God could hear.

Diane Ranker Riesen

Those Eyes

Photographer: Rachael M. Kaufman-Martin

Those Eyes

Within those tender, love-filled eyes ~
I see God's mighty hand....
I wished to see a miracle... and NOW, I understand.
How perfect can God's crafting be ~
what power I can see...
Inside those perfect, baby eyes.... I see God's Majesty.

A very special magic... lives in a tiny child ~
A power to show such innocence-
a sweetness, soft and mild.
I never feel more close to God...
then when a child is near;
The orchestra of Angels... is what I always hear.

We all strive to see Heaven ~ the earth can be so tough;
there's just so many struggles...
and trials so very rough......
But, all it takes is one quick look - into a baby's eyes ~
to answer all your questions.... and to erase all your 'why's.

Diane Ranker Riesen

Today

Today…. for no good reason… just
take the time to smile ~
take time from all your worries, and sit for just awhile.
There's nothing more important than
'warming' up your soul…
Don't miss the chance to feel the joy ..
that makes your spirit whole.

Diane Ranker Riesen

Too Soon

Photographer: Cindy Shuff Peacock

Too Soon

Do I dare to wish so sweetly…..
or was that my only chance?
Could I ever love another; or was that my only 'dance'?
Our time was stopped so quickly~
and I know that he's above…
Is there really someone else here.. that I could truly love?

I'll never love the same again;
and that's how it should be ~
But, I wonder if you have someone ~
to share his life with me.
I was so blessed to feel true love; as short as it had been;
And, I will wait to sense 'Your' lead ~
'if I could love again."

Diane Ranker Riesen

Unique

Photographer: Mary Beth Watson

Unique

I never cease to be amazed….. when I go to the beach;
Each time I find another unique marvel in my reach ~
I'm breathless at the beauty of the grains of sand I hold ~
Yet, in that sand..are many treasures waiting to behold.

Two tiny children on the shore are
squealing with delight…
Their little hands have dug the sand
and found shells in their sight!
They run to show their parents all the
treasures they had found ~
then put those pearly gifts up to their ears to hear a sound.

I have that same child-like delight…
in finding different shells ~
as new ones show up on the beach
from waters, as they swell.
The colors are incredible ~ they join,
and merge, and twirl …
I find I'm just as happy as that little boy and girl!

I can't help but be mesmerized by
what our God has done ~
He took the time to make each shell..
so beautiful…. each one!
If God's great talent makes the beach
so special in each way…..
I can't imagine what our Heaven's home will be one day.

Diane Ranker Riesen

We are America

Photographer: Brianne Christman

We Are America

(9/11/2001)

Our mighty land of hopes and truths; built strong upon a
people's dream,
Will rise above these darkened clouds ~ will sing above the
thundering scream.
With all our strength, we will not fall... we shall not lay
down ~ lost and done;
for we will stand against this force; and in the end, will
overcome.

~We Are America~

We shall not flinch at our demise; nor end our dreams
amidst the cries;
We shall endure despite the loss ~ to wave our flags, at any
cost.
Within these dark, unchartered days; our souls will wash
away the stain;
A rebirth shall embrace our land... and we will be made
'whole' again.

~We Are America~

We each shall mourn; and mourn we must ~ this time
    engulfed with days unjust;
But, then those tears will clear our view... to see a future,
    fresh and new ~
We, the people, stand as one... our country built on love;
No outward foe can crush us ~ we are held by 'Him' above.

~We Are America~

Diane Ranker Riesen

What If

What if Heaven came to Earth; and we could really see…
what our lives will feel like…….in our 'Eternity"?
What if, for one moment, we saw God in the flesh;
would we be better in the end; or do we need this 'test'?

Our 'Faith' is what defines us… and
our strength to carry on~
I think God always knew we'd need
this test to make us strong.
We need to have this struggle ~ God
knew the fate of man….
He's always known the end result..
and purpose of HIs plan.

We can't appreciate the 'joy'…. that one day we will feel ~
Unless we've known the heartaches..
and know that 'pain' is real.
The sorrows that we go through; the
lessons that we learn….
will make things even clearer…
when our God 'does' return.

The miracle of Heaven ~ will all be realized;
and every perfect piece of it…will lay before our eyes.
Sometimes it takes great sorrow- to
understand what's best ~
Sometimes it takes real heartache…to truly love the 'rest'.

When all our years have ended ~ and we face 'eternity';
Our faith will be rewarded, and then we'll finally 'see'…
God's plan was always perfect; and
we'll enter through the gate ~
to see that our eternity was always worth the wait!

Diane Ranker Riesen

When Hearts Will Cry

In Memory of Larry Baumgartner

When Hearts Will Cry

THOUGH NEVER CAN THE TIME BE RIGHT..
TO SAY 'GOOD-BYE' OR BID GOOD-NIGHT;
THE TIME ARRIVES FOR EACH TO FEEL –
WHEN DEATH DRAWS NEAR,
WITH MUCH TO STEAL.

BUT, FEAR NOT SORROW, NOR THE PAIN~
IT'S NORMAL TRIALS WILL COME AGAIN.
NO LIFE IS BROUGHT TO US REVEALED~
WITHOUT THE CRUSH OF LOSS CONCEALED.

CHERISH EVERY SECOND THROUGH ~
REPLACE THE EMPTINESS IN 'YOU',
TO LET PAIN TAKE THE JOY AWAY.....
WOULD LET 'DEATH' WIN,
AND 'LOVE' NOT STAY.

Diane Ranker Riesen

Why?

Do you think I never see you?
---that I cannot feel your pain?
I am always right beside you---
and I'll never leave again.

I can watch all things from Heaven ~
I am never far away;
I wish that I could show you ~
that I'm with you every day.

Do you think I'd do things differently?
Would I try to fight God's plan?
On earth I would have wondered....
from 'here', I understand.

Each sadness that you're given ~
and every tear you cry....
Seems wrong from where you are now ~
But I have no questions, "Why"?

Be strong, my special loved ones.....
Your Faith can get you through ~
and then, when you're in Heaven...
You'll understand it, too!

Diane Ranker Riesen

Wings of Night

Artist: Christine Vera Mundschau

Wings of Night

My slumber brings me wings for flight…
To skim the perfect waves of night;
My soul can wander 'midst the air-
My dreams can take me anywhere.

And as I breathe the darkened sky…
My heart takes rest; my worries die -
And for that brief but precious time..
My life is right; the world is mine.

Oh, but that each day could be
As sweet as evening is to me.
But, morn arrives, as always will -
And I must wait again… until ~

The sun takes rest, the moon awakes;
Each star takes light and darkness breaks.
Then, once again my spirit flies….
My dreams unfold amongst the skies.

Diane Ranker Riesen

Wisdom

Photographer: Angela Krueger & Colleen Bush

Wisdom

The older that I get in years... the less I understand;
Why did I rush through every day and miss the gifts at
    hand?
My days were always hurried; and I tried to do so much....
that I missed the simple miracles that I could see and touch.

If I could go back thirty years... and change one simple
    thing ~
I'd worry less, I'd stop to rest, I'd laugh much more and
    'sing'!
I thought I had to 'prove' myself, and be who others
    thought ~
..that I was judged by how I looked, and what I had and
    bought.

The one great gift of growing years is that you realize.......
your worth was never based on what is seen through other's
    'eyes'.
I've learned the only 'real' truth is what my soul would feel ~
and when I felt that inner joy... I knew my life was 'real'.

If I had one wish I could grant, one special hope to share ~
I'd pray we all learn early on... that 'Peace' is everywhere.
Love is all God really wants, He doesn't need the rest.
A simple life that spreads sweet 'joy'..is what is really BEST!

Diane Ranker Riesen

Words From Heaven

Photographer: Jessica Hunter

Words From Heaven

(What My Parents Would Say)

"Okay, my dear, now stop the tears;
I know you'll miss me through the years~
But, if I know you'll be okay...
then this is where I want to stay.

I wish I could reach through the clouds ~
to kiss your cheek and say out loud;
'Fear not at all, for I have won,
God blessed me for the good I've done'.

Yes, I have you on earth I know;
and when it's time for you to go ~
You'll understand as you draw close...
that 'this' is where you'll love the most!

I watch you all through every day;
and pray for joy in every way.
I just don't want a saddened face ~
just put my love back, in it's place.

I've always felt that life was best ~
when all my families' lives were blessed;
So live each day the way I taught,
for I have found what I have sought."

Diane Ranker Riesen

Worry

Photographer: Sydni Claunch

Worry

When my heart is burdened heavy ~
with a mind of worried thoughts.....
when nothing can relieve me;
and I feel that I am lost....

I try to take a moment
to close my eyes and pray.....
but all my crowded thinking;
just steals the time away.

I know that God is with me,
I know His truth is real......
but my human self is fully flawed;
I can't help how I feel.

When I feel helpless, weak and tired -
and these moments steal my day;
I take whatever time I need,
to calm my mind and pray.

I'll always have these broken times,
my earthly self is weak.
But, very deeply in my soul...
where no words need to speak ~

I know My God is listening;
I know He understands....
And even when my mind can't think;
I know I'm in "His" hands.

I remember that HIS truth is real…
I know He wants what's best.
These truths help my confusion-
and I lean on Him for rest.

He'll answer every prayer I seek ~
I know He'll do what's best;
and with that truth, my worries calm..
and I find strength to rest.

Diane Ranker Riesen

Years Gone By

Photographer: Maria Wahl

Years Gone By

I remember the halls…I remember the sounds ~
of the voices conversing; and the friendships we found.
All the books and the classes - the days that would fly;
I can hardly believe all those years have gone by.

I think we can all close our eyes and pretend~
and in a few moments… We're back there again.
We're sitting at desks and exchanging the news…
Enjoying our triumphs, and sharing our blues.

We were there for each other, through
thick and through thin;
as we started the paths that our lives would begin.

But, strange as it seems…. It's not "Us" anymore -
Who follow the schedules and race on the floor.
---it's our CHILDREN who follow our legacy there~
who trace our old footsteps…. Whose
memories we'll share.

One lesson I've learned as I've grown on in years……
What gives me most pleasure - what brings joyful tears;
are the triumph's MY children attain now, instead…
It means so much more than what I'd done ahead.

I think when you're younger ~ you search for the dreams…
That will benefit "YOU" - and not others, it seems.
But, you learn as you age…and some
wisdom breaks through~
That the trophies worth winning--have 'little' with YOU!

It's the truths and the love that you gave on the way.....
So that, others, in turn.... Can repeat them some day.
No fame, or no money...no 'beauty' of face ~~
Can replace the rewards that love puts in their place.

Each day is a new one...with memories to grow~
Each one's a "beginning", with much more to know!

Just remember each morning - to cherish each day;
Take time for what matters....... and relish the 'way'.
Spend less time at work ~ and play all the while;
Forget how to worry ---- and trust with each trial.

May all of your days be as good as the last ~
embrace each new journey; and cherish the past.
Keep strong, and be healthy, stay happy ~ and then;
Your soul will be filled with great memories, my friend.

Diane Ranker Riesen

You Remind Me

You remind me of a 'seashell'.... no
"two" are quite the same ~
You remind me how I used to love
to dance out in the rain!

You remind me of a 'starfish"... that
drifts upon the shore -
and just when my heart feels complete...
I find I love you more!

You remind me of the 'moonbeams' that
sparkle through the night ~
and the warmth I feel so sweetly as
I stand in soft sunlight.

You remind me of a 'lion'... whose
strength is never done ~
and when I need some comfort... I
know that "you're" the one.

You remind me of a 'butterfly'... so delicate and small ~
Yet, always there to help me... and catch me if I fall.

You remind me of a 'preacher'..
who stands before a crowd ~
and has no fear to speak his truth...
and shout his 'Faith' out loud.

You remind me of a 'soldier'... who fights until the end ~
and shows the strength of true Faith...
that others just pretend.

You remind me of a 'Willow tree'...
whose branches bend and sway ~
a gentleness that covers you... and power when you pray.

So many 'friends' are ALL of these...
I wish that "I" could be ~
That's why I deeply cherish 'you'...
you make a "better" me!

Diane Ranker Riesen

Epilogue

I'm just like you. I have days when everything seems to be great. And then, I have days when it seems like the world is crashing down around me, and I feel overwhelmed. You and I aren't alone.

When I have those times that I struggle so hard to understand the reason for all the sadness in the world, I feel guilty. My 'faith' is always within me, and I feel weak for not completely handing my worries over to God and trusting Him that everything happens for a reason. But, I've learned that I shouldn't feel guilty. And neither should YOU.

You and I don't see things from God's vantage point. We are human beings who have the weaknesses that we will always have while we're here on earth. Having doubts and times of weakness are always going to test us. If Christ, Himself, could call out to God when He was nearing His death on the cross, then why would we think we could ever be any different?

I've learned that my 'Faith' doesn't shelter me from the weaknesses that all humans have. I know that my faith will carry me through my trials; but, I will always struggle. God understands.

Eight of the most powerful words in the world to me are from Psalm 46:10, "Be Still and know that I am God." In my heart, this simple phrase is the most beautiful piece of poetry I've ever read. Those words alone sum up what my poetry mean to me. When I steal away to the quiet place deep inside of me, the words of my poems just seem to whisper out to me.

All of us can have those special talks with God. I'm not special at all. God uses so many different ways to speak to each of us in our own unique way. You may feel God most close to you when you're walking through a woods, or listening to music. He may speak to you more clearly when you're doing some of the most mundane chores of your week. Wherever you are, whatever you're doing, just 'be still'. God's always right there. We just all need to quiet our lives long enough to hear Him in all the different ways He comes to us.

None of us are going to get through this life without pain and heartache. Some people have much more sorrow than others, but, we all have struggles.

No matter how confused, angry, or helpless you may feel, there will come a time when you see some light at the end of the tunnel. We won't understand the reason why certain things have happened but, with faith, we will be able to make it through our lives until the day we do get to see everything from God's view.

Diane Ranker Riesen